8/17

P9-EJK-745

♫ ...with a little help from my friends... ♫

For Geoff, Sue, Abby, Hannah, Nick & Polly, with love. ♫

Text and illustrations copyright © 1986 by Jill Murphy. All rights reserved.
This book, or parts thereof, may not be reproduced in any form without permission
in writing from the publisher.
A PaperStar Book, published in 1999 by Penguin
Putnam Books for Young Readers, 345 Hudson Street, New York, NY 10014.
PaperStar is a registered trademark of The Putnam Berkley Group, Inc.
The PaperStar logo is a trademark of The Putnam Berkley Group, Inc.
Originally published in 1986 by Walker Books, London.
First American edition published in 1986 by G. P. Putnam's Sons.
Printed in Shenzhen, Guangdong, China
Library of Congress number: 86-643
ISBN 13 : 978-0-698-11787-7
13 15 16 14 12

Five Minutes' Peace

Jill Murphy

PaperStar

Penguin Young Readers Group

The children were having breakfast.
This was not a pleasant sight.

Mrs. Large took a tray from the cupboard.
She set it with a teapot, a milk jug, her
favorite cup and saucer, a plate of
marmalade toast and a leftover cake
from yesterday. She stuffed the morning
paper into her pocket and sneaked off
toward the door.

"Where are you going with that tray, Mom?" asked Laura.

"To the bathroom," said Mrs. Large.

"Why?" asked the other two children.

"Because I want five minutes' peace from all of *you*," said Mrs. Large. "That's why."

"Can *we* come?" asked Lester as they trailed
   up the stairs behind her.
"No," said Mrs. Large, "you can't."
"What shall *we* do then?" asked Laura.
"You can play," said Mrs. Large. "Downstairs.
   By yourselves. And keep an eye on the baby."
"I'm *not* a baby," muttered the little one.

Mrs. Large ran a deep, hot bath.
She emptied half a bottle of bubble bath
into the water, plunked on her shower cap
and got in. She poured herself a cup of tea
and lay back with her eyes closed.
It was heaven.

"Can I play you my tune?" asked Lester.

Mrs. Large opened one eye. "Must you?" she asked.

"I've been practicing," said Lester. "You told me to.
Can I? Please, just for one minute."

"Go on then," sighed Mrs. Large.

So Lester played. He played "Twinkle, Twinkle,
Little Star" three and a half times.

In came Laura. "Can I read you a page from
my reading book?" she asked.

"*No*, Laura," said Mrs. Large. "Go on, *all* of you,
off downstairs."

"You let Lester play his tune," said Laura.

"I heard. You like him better than me. It's not fair."

"Oh, don't be silly, Laura," said Mrs. Large.

"Go *on* then. Just *one* page."

So Laura read. She read four and a half pages
of "Little Red Riding Hood."

In came the little one with a trunkful of toys.
"For *you*!" he beamed, flinging them all
into the bath water.
"Thank you, dear," said Mrs. Large weakly.

"Can I see the cartoons in the paper?" asked Laura.

"Can I have the cake?" asked Lester.

"Can I get in with you?" asked the little one.

Mrs. Large groaned.

In the end they *all* got in. The
little one was in such a hurry that
he forgot to take off his pajamas.

Mrs. Large got out. She dried herself, put on her bathrobe and headed for the door.

"Where are you going *now*, Mom?" asked Laura.

"To the kitchen," said Mrs. Large.

"Why?" asked Lester.

"Because I want five minutes' peace from all of *you*," said Mrs. Large. "That's why."

And off she went downstairs,
where she had three minutes
and forty-five seconds of peace
before they all came to join her.